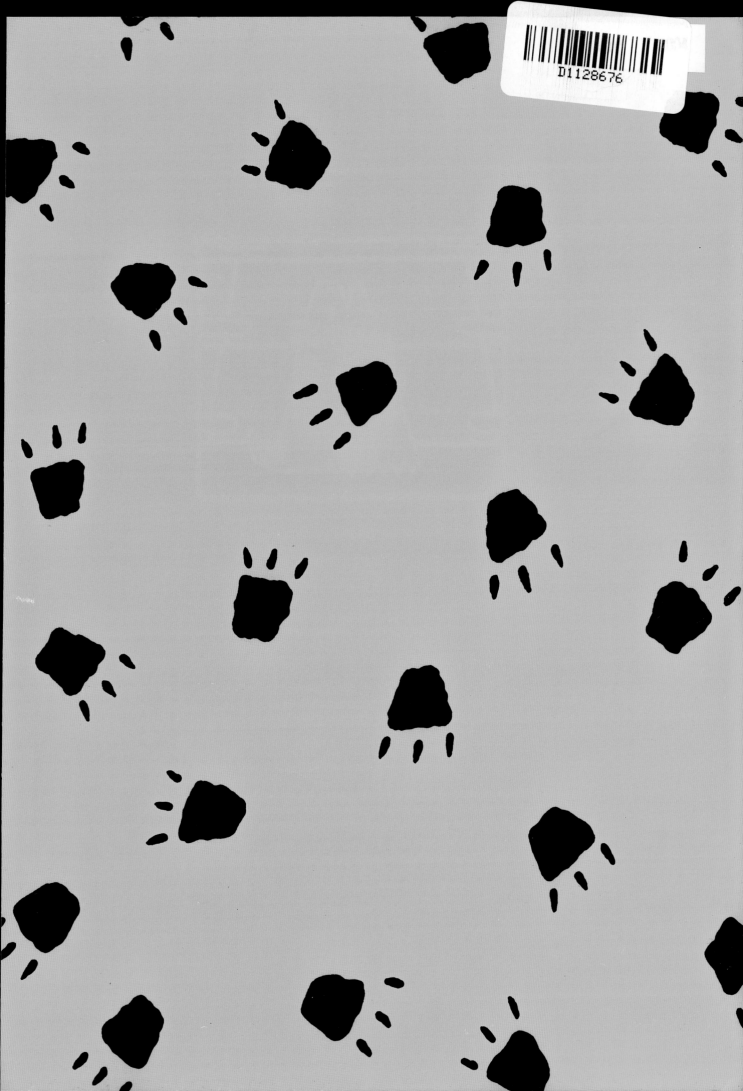

For my Mum and Dad

—Nicola Edwards

Text and illustrations copyright © 2002 by Nicola Edwards
Style and design copyright © 2002 by Chrysalis Children's Books Limited
The Chrysalis Building, Bramley Road, London W10 6SP
An imprint of Chrysalis Books Group plc

First published in the United States in 2004 by
Running Press Kids, an imprint of
Running Press Book Publishers
125 South Twenty-second Street
Philadelphia, Pennsylvania 19103-4399

Printed in Singapore

9   8   7   6   5   4   3   2   1
Digit on the right indicates the number of this printing

Library of Congress Control Number: 2003093020

ISBN: 0-7624-1725-0

Designed by: Scott Gibson
Edited by: Helen Mortimer
Typography: Baxter

This book may be ordered by mail from the publisher.
Please include $2.50 for postage and handling.
But try your bookstore first!

Visit us on the web!
www.runningpress.com

Goodnight Baxter

by Nicola Edwards

RUNNING PRESS
KIDS
PHILADELPHIA·LONDON

"**Surprise!**" said Daddy
as he opened his jacket
and out popped a puppy.

"I'm going to call him Baxter," said Charlie. Baxter licked Charlie's face.

Baxter and Charlie played all afternoon with the toys that Daddy had bought from the pet store.

At bedtime, Charlie put Baxter in his basket.

He gave Baxter
a goodnight kiss.
Then he went upstairs.

Baxter closed his eyes and tried to sleep...

in his basket...

on top of his basket...

under his basket...

over the side of his basket.

He even tried leaning
against his basket.
But it was no good.
He just couldn't sleep.

He had to go upstairs
and find Charlie.

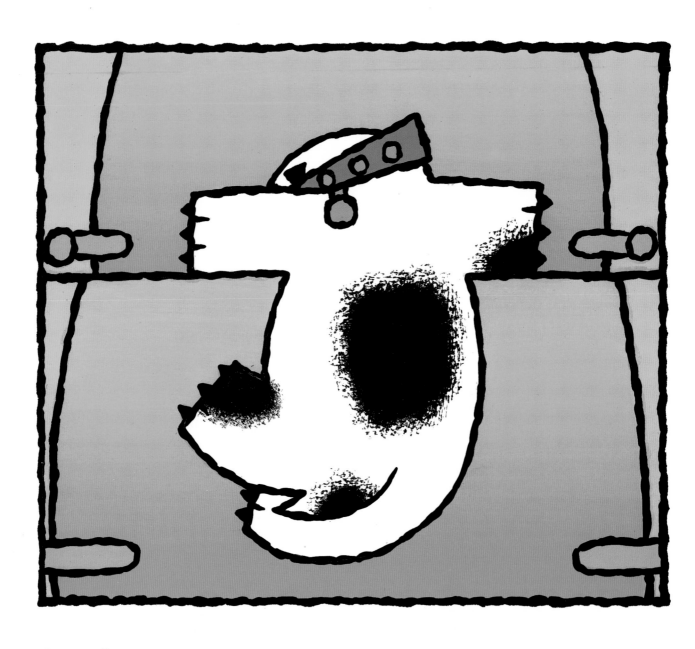

But every time Baxter
tried to climb the stairs..

he tumbled back down.

So he sat at the bottom
of the stairs and barked.

Charlie tiptoed quietly downstairs with a warm, cosy blanket for Baxter.

But Baxter kicked it off...

jumped out of his basket...

and barked for Charlie.

So Charlie carried his favorite teddy bear downstairs for Baxter.

But Baxter tossed it away...

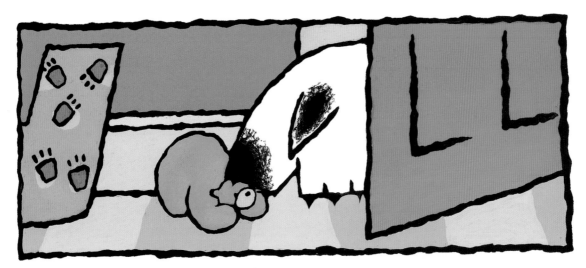

jumped out of his basket...

and barked and barked for Charlie.

Charlie even found his old pacifier and took it downstairs for Baxter.

But Baxter spat it out...

jumped out of his basket...

and barked and barked and barked for Charlie.

But this time Charlie
didn't wake up.
He was fast asleep.

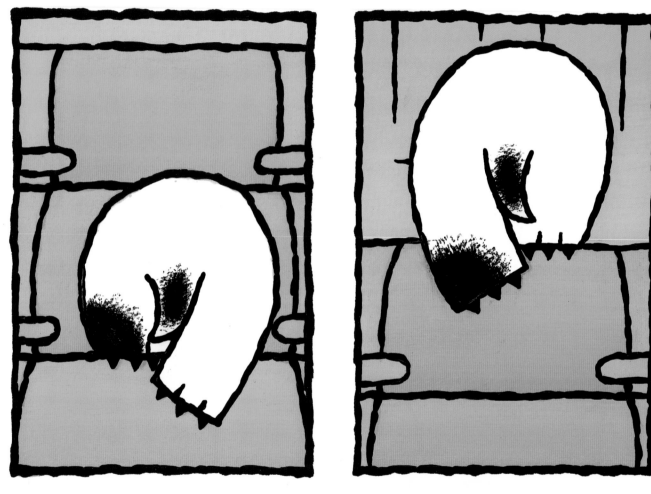

So Baxter wobbled and
stumbled up the stairs...
until he reached the top.

He pushed open Charlie's door with his nose.

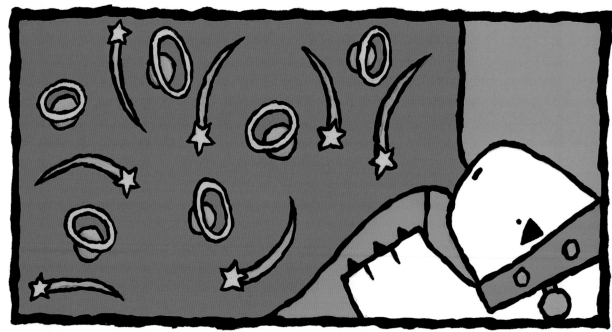

Baxter gave Charlie's blanket a little tug...

he put his wet nose on Charlie's hand...

he even licked one of Charlie's ears... until Charlie woke up.

Because Baxter didn't want a blanket... or a teddy... or a pacifier...

He wanted Charlie!

"Goodnight, Baxter!" said Charlie. And they both fell fast asleep.

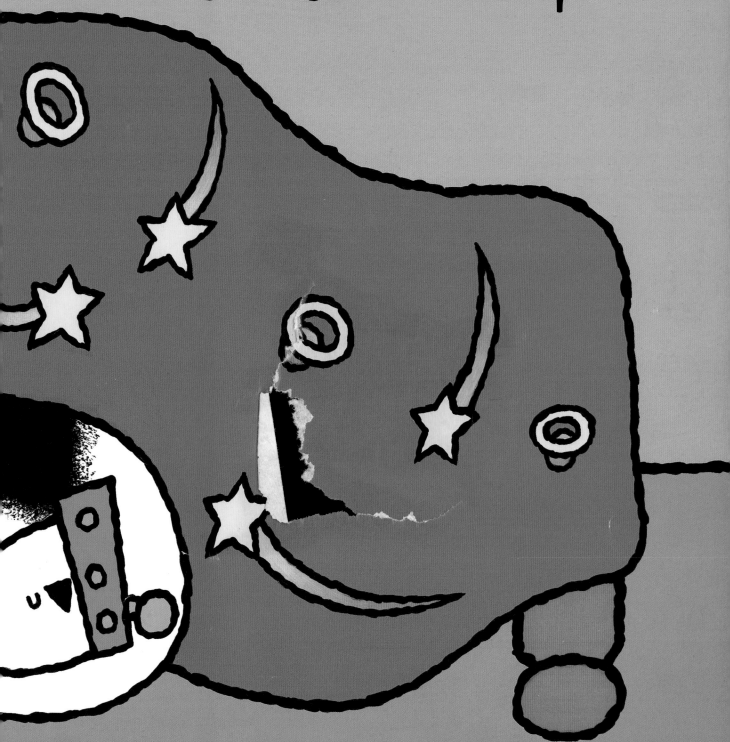